ADVENTURES of the
Steampunk Pirates

Clash of the Rival Robots

To the Dread Captain Olwen and
Gruff the cabin boy – GPJ

To Thelma – FAD

STRIPES PUBLISHING
An imprint of Little Tiger Press
1 The Coda Centre, 189 Munster Road,
London SW6 6AW

A paperback original
First published in Great Britain in 2015

Text copyright © Gareth P. Jones, 2015
Illustrations copyright © Artful Doodlers, 2015
Cover typeface courtesy of www.shutterstock.com

ISBN: 978-1-84715-606-8

A CIP catalogue record for this book is available
from the British Library.

Printed and bound in the UK.

10 9 8 7 6 5 4 3 2 1

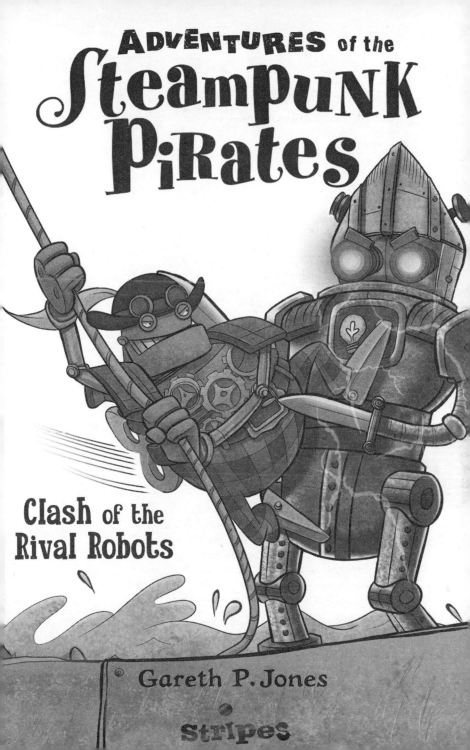

WANTED

DEAD OR ALIVE!
(or smashed into little bits and delivered in boxes)

The crew of the *Leaky Battery* the STEAMPUNK PIRATES for piracy, looting and treason.

Sixteen scurrilous scallywags in total, including their four officers:

CAPTAIN CLOCKHEART
Hot-headed leader of the Steampunk Pirates. He is unpredictable and dangerous on account of a loose valve sending too much steam to his head.

FIRST MATE MAINSPRING
Operated by clockwork, he is at his most devious when overly wound up.

QUARTERMASTER LEXI
Fitted with a catalogue of information, he is the cleverest (if not the bravest) of the bunch.

MR GADGE
His various arm attachments include all kinds of devilish weaponry and fighting equipment.

A REWARD OF
THREE THOUSAND POUNDS
is offered for anyone who captures this crew of loathsome looters and returns them to their rightful owner, the King of England.

We are the Steampunk Pirates,
We're fearsome, fierce and strong,
A man named Swift did make us,
With hammer, screws and tong,
He forged our skin from iron,
But, friends, it won't be long,
Until we mould,
New parts from gold,
And sing a golden song,
(A song!)
We'll sing a golden song!

CHAPTER 1

In which the *Leaky Battery*
is caught in a storm,
Quartermaster Lexi feels
sick and our heroes spot an
albatross … of sorts.

The storm had come out of nowhere. Huge
waves crashed over the side of the *Leaky
Battery*. The ship rocked back and forth, and
the crew clung on for dear life.

"Reef that sail and batten down the
hatches," cried Captain Clockheart. The hand
of the clock in his chest whirled around.

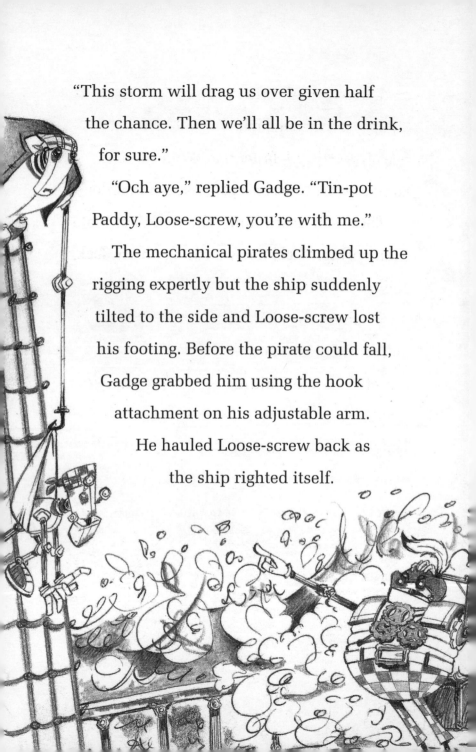

"This storm will drag us over given half the chance. Then we'll all be in the drink, for sure."

"Och aye," replied Gadge. "Tin-pot Paddy, Loose-screw, you're with me."

The mechanical pirates climbed up the rigging expertly but the ship suddenly tilted to the side and Loose-screw lost his footing. Before the pirate could fall, Gadge grabbed him using the hook attachment on his adjustable arm.

He hauled Loose-screw back as the ship righted itself.

"Quickly now," cried Captain Clockheart. "If any of you metal marauders fall in that ocean, you'll sink faster than a bucketful of cannonballs! Now, let's get this ship in order."

"**Click**, you heard him," shouted First Mate Mainspring. "**Tick**, tie everything down. **Tock**, secure the ship."

"Captain, the chances of surviving this storm…" Quartermaster Lexi's words were cut off by a wave hitting the deck. When the water drained away, it left a flapping fish caught in the word-wheel on Lexi's head. "Help me! Get it out! I don't like it…"

Captain Clockheart flicked the fish back into the ocean with the tip of his cutlass as another enormous wave came down on top of them. Gadge climbed down the rigging and dropped on to the deck. "The sails are reefed, Captain."

"**Click**, everything is secure," said First Mate Mainspring.

"Then it's time we got down below and sat this one out," said Captain Clockheart.

The Steampunk Pirates hurriedly followed their captain below deck.

"Oh dear, oh dear," said Quartermaster Lexi, holding his hand to his mouth.

"There's no need to worry, Lexi," said Pendle the cabin boy.[1] "The *Leaky Battery* has survived worse than this."

---

1. Pendle the cabin boy was the only human crewmember of the *Leaky Battery*. She was unlike most cabin boys for two reasons: a) She had a flair for engineering. b) She was a girl.

"I know that," said Lexi, "but all this rocking is making me feel rather queasy."

"I didn't know you lot could even get sick," said Pendle.

"It's the oil and the water getting mixed up together," replied Lexi. "Oh dear." He ran to a corner and sent a stomachful of oily water into a bucket.

"Better out than in, laddie." Gadge chuckled and patted Lexi on the back.

"Is everyone accounted for?" asked Captain Clockheart.

"I think so," replied Pendle, "although I haven't seen Twitter in a while."

Hearing his name, the mechanical bird fluttered down from the rafters and landed on Pendle's shoulder. "Safe and sound!" he squawked. "Safe and sound!"

The storm raged against the ship for several hours, but as the sun was setting in the blood-red sky, the wind calmed down and the rain eased off. Captain Clockheart opened the hatch and led the others up on deck. He gazed at the torn sails and broken crossbeams. The ship's wheel was hanging on by a thread.

"Oh dear, oh dear," said Lexi, looking at the mess.

"The old *Battery* has taken quite a battering," said Captain Clockheart.

"**Click**, we must repair her. **Tick**, if we hit another storm in this state, **tock**, she'll be the *Sunken Battery*," said First Mate Mainspring.

"We'll need to find new wood to repair her properly," said Pendle.

"Och, then it's a safe port to drop anchor that we'll want," said Gadge.

"Aye. Now, where are we?" Captain Clockheart shielded his eyes and surveyed the horizon.

"Maybe that albatross will lead us to land," said Pendle, peering through a telescope.

Lexi's word-wheel turned and a card clicked into place. "Albatross," he said. "A large seabird. If shot down, it is believed to bring bad luck to sailors."

"**Click**, it's coming this way," said First Mate Mainspring. "**Tick**, I've never seen a bird catch the sunlight like that. **Tock**, it's almost as though..."

"It's made of metal," said Pendle.

"Metal?" Captain Clockheart snatched the telescope off Pendle. "Why, I believe you're right, lad."

"Shoot it down!" squawked Twitter.

"It's in range." Gadge selected his rifle attachment.

"Lower your weapon, Mr Gadge. Let's find out what this shiny seabird wants," said Captain Clockheart.

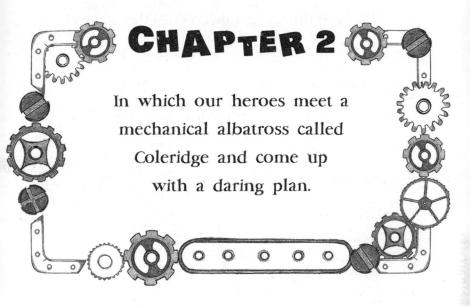

CHAPTER 2

In which our heroes meet a
mechanical albatross called
Coleridge and come up
with a daring plan.

The mechanical bird's large wings allowed
it to glide elegantly through the air. Twitter
watched jealously as it flew down, leaving
a white trail of vapour in its wake. It landed
gracefully on the side of the ship.

"Blimey, am I glad to find you lot! I've
been flying for weeks. Do a bird a favour and

give us something to nibble on, would you?"
said the albatross.

Captain Clockheart popped open his
stomach, pulled out a piece of glowing
coal and threw it into the air. The albatross
jumped up and caught it in its beak. "Ah,
that's better. Thanks. The name's Coleridge,
but me friends call me Ridgey."

Twitter hopped along the rail.

"All right, little fella. Admiring the old
wingspan, are you? That's three metres of
wing right there, that is." Ridgey stretched
out his huge wings.

"Show off!" muttered Twitter. "Show off!"

Pendle leaned forward to inspect the bird. "A steam-powered albatross. Who made you, then?" she asked.

"The same geezer that made this lot. Old Swifty of course," responded Ridgey.

"Mr Richmond Swift?" said Pendle.

"Our creator!" gasped Gadge.

"That no-good scallywag," snarled Captain Clockheart. "He made us as servants for the king. If it hadn't been for Pendle, we'd still be carrying trays of party food and washing dishes."

"Ah, but without him we wouldn't have our lives at all," said Lexi. "Ours is a complicated relationship, similar to that between—"

Captain Clockheart whacked Lexi on the back of the head, shutting him down.

"I don't like complicated things." He turned to Ridgey. "So why did he make *you*, then?"

"I was a guard bird at the Tower of London."

"You're a long way from London now," said Pendle.

Ridgey looked at the cabin boy meaningfully. "So are you, chum."

"We're not talking about me," Pendle replied quickly. "Why are you here?"

"I'm here for the same reason as the rest of you," said Ridgey. "Freedom."

"**Click**, how do you know about us?" asked Mainspring.

"Know about you? Swifty used to go on about you lot all the time. He was furious when you took off. As an apology to the king, he created me to guard the crown jewels."

A jet of steam escaped from Captain Clockheart's head as he moved closer to the albatross. "Say that again."

"What? The crown jewels?" said Ridgey.

There was a fluttering noise as Lexi came back to life and his word-wheel started up again. "The crown jewels," he said. "A collection of valuable items owned by the King of England." He looked around, confused. "I say, I really wish you wouldn't switch me off like that."

"Never mind that," said the captain. He turned back to the albatross. "Tell me more about this treasure."

"It's all kept in a room at the top of a big tower surrounded by armed guards," replied Ridgey. "No one in their right mind would think of *stealing* it... That is, unless they knew someone who could get them inside. Someone like me."

"We like the sound of a room full of treasure, don't we, lads?" The captain's clock hand whizzed around excitedly.

The crew cheered but Lexi looked concerned. "The Tower of London is the most well protected place in the whole of England."

"Which means they'll never expect it," said Gadge.

"What about the damage from the storm?" asked Pendle. "Shouldn't we get the ship in working order first?"

"We'll repair her on the way," said Captain Clockheart. "Quartermaster Lexi, plot a course for England."

"Aye, sir, although with a broken rudder

and torn sails it may take longer than it should," replied Lexi.

First Mate Mainspring sighed. "**Click**, and so our captain puts us all in danger again. **Tick**, sailing a broken ship into a potential death trap. **Tock**, when will he learn?"

"Don't listen to old clickerty-tick-tocks," said Ridgey. "You're Captain Clockheart, ain't you? Them crown jewels are as good as yours."

The captain patted Ridgey then fed him a handful of wood shavings from his pocket. "Twitter, you could learn a lot from this albatross. Now, let's get some wind in those sails, lads. We're off to England!"

Twitter flew up to the crow's nest to sulk while the captain ordered the crew to work.

Pendle followed Lexi to the ship's

compass. Like everything else on the ship it had been badly damaged by the storm.

"I don't like this one bit," said Pendle. "I don't trust that albatross and this ship needs a lot of work before it can outrun one of the duke's warships."

"I quite agree," said Lexi. "But you know what the captain is like once he gets an idea in that tin-pot head of his." The wheel on his head clicked as it turned. "Even if it is an idea that will most likely get us all melted down … dismantled … killed."

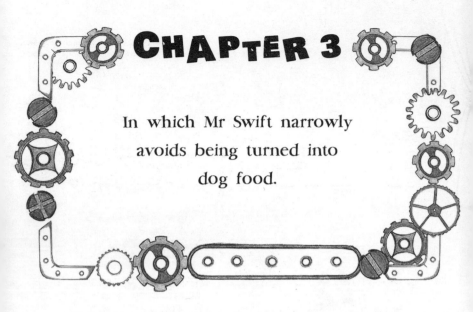

CHAPTER 3

In which Mr Swift narrowly
avoids being turned into
dog food.

Usually, if a king gets off his throne, picks up
a sword and asks you to kneel before him it
means you are about to be knighted – but this
was not the case for Mr Richmond Swift.

The king waggled his sword threateningly
at the white-haired engineer and three
vicious-looking corgis growled at him.

"Mr Swift, give me one good reason why I shouldn't run you through and turn you into dog food." The dogs barked excitedly at this.

"I can give you three good reasons," replied Mr Swift.

"Go on."

"Firstly, the way we fight wars is changing. You will need my inventions when you go to war against the French."

"You're not the only steam engineer in England," stated the king. "What's your

second reason?" He prodded Mr Swift's shirt with the tip of his sword, while one of the dogs sniffed his feet.

"Secondly, I have recently put into action a plan to bring the Steampunk Pirates to justice."

"I'll believe that when I see it. What is the third reason that I shouldn't feed you to my dogs?"

"Er…" Mr Swift thought fast. "I had a rather spicy meat pie last night and I fear it would affect my flavour. It wouldn't suit your animals' refined tastes, I'm sure."

The king lowered his sword. "Yes, they are quite fussy eaters." The dogs looked disappointed and Mr Swift looked extremely relieved. "So tell me about your plan to bring in these runaway servants of mine.

I've just increased the reward for their capture. It's very embarrassing knowing they're out there, plundering my ships and making a fool out of me."

"Well, so far all the attempts to capture them have involved your men chasing after the pirates and fighting them on their own terms. My plan, on the other hand, will deliver them right into your hands."

"What do you mean?"

"I recently created a mechanical albatross, which I sent off to locate the Steampunk Pirates. The bird has been tasked with persuading this bunch of escapees to steal the crown jewels."

The king gripped his sword tightly. "You mean, *my* crown jewels?" he stated. "You're using *my* crown jewels as bait?"

Mr Swift laughed nervously. "You have nothing to worry about, Your Majesty. My plan is completely foolproof. You see, it is my belief that to *catch* a machine one must *use* a machine. Behold—"

"I do hate it when you say that word," interrupted the king.

"Then ... allow me to introduce you to ... the Electrical Soldiers."

At the other end of the room, a large door burst open and two huge mechanical men entered. The sound of their metal joints echoed off the walls as they walked along. They were taller than the Steampunk Pirates, with cone-like heads. Instead of the crackling fire and hiss of a combustion engine, they made a buzzing noise and sparks flew as they moved.

"Tesla and Faraday are made of a metal ten times stronger than the pirates," Mr Swift explained proudly. "They have been fitted with the very latest fighting equipment. As you can see, each arm includes a fully operational bayonet, complete with reloading barrels and self-sharpening swords."

The corgis hid under the throne and the king dropped his sword in astonishment. "What is this word, 'electrical'?"

"It is a new method of generating power. It is my belief that one day everything will be electric. From street lamps to your own trousers…"

"My trousers!" exclaimed the king.

"Well, maybe not your trousers," said Mr Swift, "but everything else. Tesla and Faraday will follow your every command. They will fight your every war."

"WE WILL OBEY," said the Electrical Soldiers together.

"Mr Swift, have you lost your mind?" cried the king. "Having created one bunch of metal monstrosities, you offer me yet more of these tiresome tin men."

"But *these* men will defeat Clockheart's crew," insisted Mr Swift.

"And what is to stop this lot turning on me as well? What is to stop them joining the Steampunk Pirates?"

"I've already thought of that," said Mr Swift. "As part of my plan I mean to learn what made Clockheart and his crew run off. That way, I will know how to avoid it happening again."

"No, no, no!" exclaimed the king. "No more inventions. If the pirates are coming to the Tower they will be captured by living, breathing soldiers."

"But it is your soldiers who have failed to capture them so far, Your Majesty."

"Are you arguing with the King of England, Mr Swift?" demanded the king.

"Of course not, Your Highness," said Mr Swift.

"Good. It is vital that the Steampunk Pirates are defeated by real men of flesh and blood. We must demonstrate that men are better than machines."

"But, Your Majesty, these Electrical Soldiers are the future of fighting. With your permission I can build an army of them."

"With my money, you mean," said the king.

"I admit it will not be cheap, but—"

"Enough." The king cut him off. "I will send a messenger to the Iron Duke and

Admiral Fussington, giving them one last chance to bring the Steampunk Pirates to justice. If they fail me again, you will have your opportunity."

"As you command, Your Majesty." Mr Swift bowed and left, with his two Electrical Soldiers behind him.

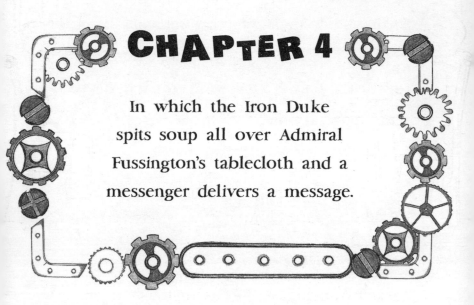

CHAPTER 4

In which the Iron Duke
spits soup all over Admiral
Fussington's tablecloth and a
messenger delivers a message.

Usually Admiral Fussington and his wife
spent mealtimes at opposite ends of the long
dining table in awkward silence. Tonight,
the Iron Duke was sitting in between them,
slurping tomato soup and dabbing his
moustache with one of Mrs Fussington's
better napkins.

"Would one care for some bread, sir?" asked Wodehouse, the Fussingtons' butler.

"This one would." The Iron Duke grabbed two rolls from the basket and dropped one into his soup. Bright orange spots splattered across the tablecloth.

"I say, didn't you have a child the last time I visited?" he asked.

"That's right. Penelope." Mrs Fussington tried not to stare at the stained tablecloth.

"But, in this household, we believe children should be seen and not heard."

"Talking of which, when *did* you last see Penelope?" asked Admiral Fussington.

"I'm not sure," replied his wife.[2]

"Which is exactly as it should be," the duke announced proudly. "My father refused to say a single word to me until I turned sixteen. Even then it was only to tell me to take my feet off the table."

Wodehouse coughed quietly.

"Yes?" said Admiral Fussington.

"One apologizes, sir, but there is a messenger here."

"Blast it, man! In the middle of dinner?" exclaimed the Iron Duke. "Tell him to go away."

---

2. The last time the Fussingtons had seen their daughter was at the king's birthday party, just before she ran off with the Steampunk Pirates and adopted the name Pendle.

"One did say words to that effect, sir, but apparently he has an urgent message from the king himself."

The Iron Duke spat out a mouthful of soup. "Well, what are you waiting for? The admiral and I will see him at once. Sorry, Mrs Fussington, but this is men's business."

"That's quite all right," she replied. "Wodehouse, show the messenger into the drawing room then be a good chap and fetch a damp sponge and some soap."

The Iron Duke and Admiral Fussington retired to the drawing room, where they found a young man with socks pulled up to his knees and shiny buttons on his jacket. He carried a bronze bugle over one shoulder and a lute over the other.

"Good evening," he said. "My name

is Ralf and I will be your messenger this evening. Please hold."

He picked up the lute and started to play. The duke and admiral looked at one another in confusion.

"Hold what?" snapped the duke.

Ralf stopped playing, pulled out an envelope from his pocket and handed it to the duke. "Please hold this. It's the message."

The duke snatched the envelope and tore it open, then read the letter inside.

"What does it say?" asked Admiral Fussington.

"It says that the Steampunk Pirates are planning to rob the Tower of London and that we are to capture them."

"Thank you for holding," said Ralf.

"Please leave your message after the beep."

"What beep?" demanded the duke.

The young man lifted the bugle and blew a high note. "That one," he said.

"Honestly. What nonsense! I can't be doing with these modern messengers," said the duke.

"Message reads: Honestly. What nonsense! I can't be doing with these modern messengers," said the messenger.

"No, blast you, man. That's not my message."

"No, blast you, man. That's not my message," repeated Ralf.

The duke grabbed the messenger by his collar and spoke through gritted teeth. "Tell the king that we will gather our men and go to the Tower at once."

The duke released the messenger, who checked his instruments were undamaged then brushed himself down. "If you would like to revise your message you can press this button." He pointed to one of the buttons on his jacket.

"Get out!" cried the duke. "Now, Admiral Fussington, we have an appointment at the Tower."

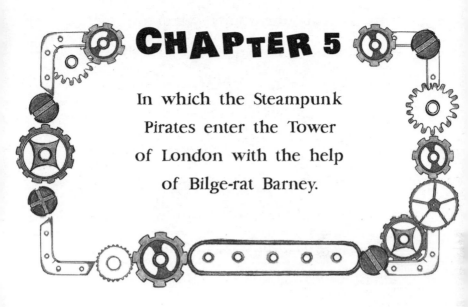

CHAPTER 5

In which the Steampunk
Pirates enter the Tower
of London with the help
of Bilge-rat Barney.

The Steampunk Pirates had not returned to England since their first daring escape from the king's birthday party. It was wetter than they remembered. The *Leaky Battery* sailed into the Thames estuary under a cloud of drizzle. A long queue of grumbling pirates stood before Pendle, waiting to have their joints oiled and their bolts tightened. She was just dealing with a particularly difficult squeaky bottom, when Captain Clockheart appeared.

"Pendle lad, you're needed below deck," he said. "Follow me."

"What about me?" said Blind Bob Bolt.

"Your bottom will have to wait," said Captain Clockheart. "I need our cabin boy below deck."

Pendle put down her oil can and followed the captain into the lowest part of the ship.

"What are we doing down in the bilge?" she asked, holding her nose to block out the stink of the water that had collected at the base of the ship.

"We're here to see Bilge-rat Barney," replied Captain Clockheart.

"Did someone say old Bilge-rat's name?"

A figure stepped out from behind a wooden beam. He was so covered in rust that big rolls of it were flaking off him. He walked with a limp and his metal had warped to give him a hunched back. He was in a far worse state than the rest of the crew.

"Aye aye, Captain." He saluted, knocking off a fresh piece of rust from above his eyes. "Hello, Pendle, I bets you'd forgotten about old Bilge-rat Barney, hadn't you?"

"Of course not," Pendle lied. "I could take a look at that rust problem of yours, if you like."

"Problem? Old Bilge-rat don't have no problem. This rust is who I am," said the pirate. "I wouldn't trade it any more than I would this rattling old head of mine." He clasped his head protectively.

"Bilge-rat has been working on a concoction that should get us into the Tower," said Captain Clockheart.

"That's right," said Bilge-rat. "Down here, I likes to spend my time mixing liquids and minerals. Sometimes they make big bangs. I likes the bangs. Sometimes they make funny smells. I don't likes the smells."

"Never mind that," said Captain Clockheart. "Tell Pendle what you've discovered."

"Old Bilge-rat has found a way to overcome all these soldiers without a single

swing of a cutlass or shot of a pistol. Watch this." He splashed through the water and strapped on to his back a pair of bolted-together barrels, with a hosepipe coming out the top. "When the two liquids in these barrels mix, they makes knockout gas," said Bilge-rat.

"What does that mean?" asked Pendle.

"Have a sniff." Bilge-rat lifted his thumbs off the end of the hosepipe, giving Pendle no choice but to breathe in the gas.

Everything went black.

When Pendle awoke, she found herself gazing up at Captain Clockheart's hissing chin. She could feel the hot metal of his hands on her back. He looked down at her and smiled. It took her a moment to remember what had happened.

"That wasn't a very nice thing to do," she said, getting to her feet.

"Sorry, lad," said the captain.

"Till now, I'd only tested it on vermin," said Bilge-rat. "We needed to test it on a human like yourself."

"You were out for twenty minutes," said Captain Clockheart, checking the clock on his chest.

"So you plan to knock out the tower guards?" said Pendle.

"That's right," replied the captain. "With this gas and Ridgey's inside knowledge, the crown jewels are as good as ours. Still, I ain't leaving nothing to chance. That's why I'm taking the whole crew."

"Including me?" said Pendle excitedly.

"No. Not you. Ridgey suggested leaving you behind to make sure the old ship is ready for our getaway. You can keep an eye on Twitter, too. We don't want his big mouth giving us away."

Pendle's voice wavered. "Everyone's going except me and Twitter?"

"It's nothing personal, lad."

"Yo ho, down below!" called Blower from the crow's nest. "We're coming into London."

There was a dense fog hanging over the River Thames as the *Leaky Battery* dropped its anchor and the entire crew climbed into two rowing boats.

Lexi's word-wheel turned and clicked. "The Tower of London," he said. "Founded in 1066 by William the Conqueror."

"I don't remember ordering a tour guide," said Ridgey.

"**Click**, the question is not when it was built. **Tick**, nor who built it. **Tock**, but how do we get in?" said Mainspring.

"The entrance to the river is known as Traitor's Gate," said Lexi. "Named because of—"

"Traitor's Gate," interrupted Captain Clockheart. "Arr, that sounds about right, don't it, lads?"

The crew cheered.

"**Click**, keep quiet," said Mainspring. "**Tick**, this is supposed to be a silent approach. **Tock**, not a boat party."

"Halt. Who goes there?" called a voice.

"Prepare the gas, Bilge-rat," ordered Captain Clockheart.

"All ready, Captain." The rusty pirate held up the hosepipe.

"I said, who approaches?" asked the voice through the gloom. "Answer or I'll fire."

When the guard's outline came into view,

Bilge-rat blasted the knockout gas at his face. He breathed it in and dropped into the water with a SPLASH!

"Good work, Bilge-rat," said Captain Clockheart. "Gadge, get that gate open."

"Aye aye, Captain." Gadge selected a bolt-cutter attachment for his arm and opened the gate.

Captain Clockheart scooped the guard out of the water with the tip of his cutlass. He lifted him up by his belt and threw him on to the riverbank.

"Now, where's the treasure?" said Captain Clockheart.

"Top of the tallest tower," said Ridgey. "I'll go and check the lie of the land."

Captain Clockheart grabbed the albatross by his legs, clamped a padlock over them and chained him to the boat.

"What are you playing at?" said Ridgey, flapping his wings.

"If you've been honest with us, then I'll be back in a minute with the treasure," said Captain Clockheart. "That's when I'll take off that padlock."

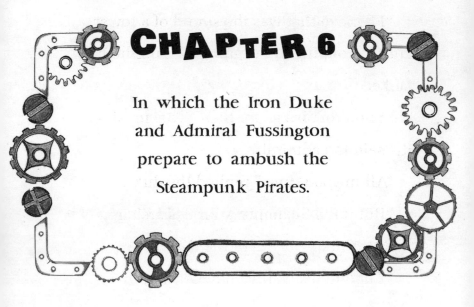

CHAPTER 6

In which the Iron Duke
and Admiral Fussington
prepare to ambush the
Steampunk Pirates.

The Iron Duke, Admiral Fussington and a
hundred armed soldiers were standing on the
other side of the Tower of London's main gate.

THUD came a sound from inside the
famous tower.

"What was that?" asked Admiral
Fussington.

"I believe that was the sound of a tower guard dropping to the ground," said the Iron Duke.

"Shouldn't we go in, then? This must be it," said the admiral.

"All in good time," replied the duke.

"But if the Steampunk Pirates are already inside, then—"

"Then it means they have a plan," interrupted the duke.

"How can you be sure?"

"Because anyone who thinks he can rob the Tower of London without a plan is a fool. We know they are not fools because they have fooled us before. A fool can only be fooled by another fool. So unless you're calling me a fool they have a plan."

"Er... Yes, sir." Admiral Fussington didn't

have the faintest idea what the duke had just said.

THUD.

"Do you know how many guards are in there?" asked the Iron Duke.

"I believe there are twenty-one on duty tonight," the admiral replied.

"Then we are nineteen thuds short of going in."

"But what if the guards are being harmed?"

"If pistols were being used we would have heard shots. If they were being run through we would have heard swordplay. No. There is something else going on here." THUD. "These men are dropping silently to the ground. No agonized screams. No pleas for mercy. But how?"

"Perhaps the pirates are sneaking up behind them and knocking them out."

THUD. THUD.

"Perhaps." The duke nodded.

THUD. THUD. THUD.

"But shouldn't we at least take a look?"

"Oh, very well." The duke walked over to a nervous-looking soldier and placed a hand on his shoulder. "You. Go and see what's going on."

THUD. THUD. THUD. THUD.

"But it's only my first day," replied the soldier.

The duke turned a deep shade of purple. "Which explains why you think it is acceptable to answer back!"

"Maybe you want to pick one of the more experienced men," pleaded the soldier.

THUD. THUD.

The Iron Duke pushed his face up so
close to the soldier's that the tips of their
noses were touching. "And maybe I want to
pick someone new and expendable!"

"What does
expendable
mean?"
asked the
soldier, his
voice wavering.

"It means that it
doesn't matter whether you come back
or not. Now, stop arguing, get your bony
bottom over the drawbridge and look inside
or you'll spend the rest of your career
hanging from your bootlaces in a cell with
no windows."

THUD. THUD. THUD.

"Yes, sir." The petrified soldier saluted then raised his gun and walked towards the tower.

THUD.

"I don't know what the world's coming to," the duke said to Admiral Fussington.

THUD. THUD. THUD.

"That's twenty-one," said Admiral Fussington. "All the guards are out."

The young soldier reached the Tower entrance. He glanced back at the others then opened a door in the gate. There was the sound of hissing and the soldier dropped to the ground with another THUD.

"Interesting," said the duke. "Did you hear that hissing noise? The pirates must be using some kind of gas to knock out the soldiers. Admiral Fussington, have one of your men run and buy smelling salts.[3] We'll dip handkerchiefs in the stuff to protect ourselves against the gas and then we'll go in and capture those Steampunk Pirates once and for all."

---

3 Smelling salts were potent chemicals used to revive people who had fainted. Not to be confused with the stuff you put on chips.

The author apologizes for this interruption, but before everything kicks off in the Tower, he wonders if you would like to catch up with Pendle.

"Twitter? Are you up there?" whispered Pendle. "Come back down."

The fog was so thick that Pendle couldn't see her hand in front of her face, let alone spot the sulking parrot up on the rigging. She was getting nervous.

"Come on, Twitter," she pleaded.

"The captain left us *both* behind. That's just the way it is sometimes."

Pendle heard the unmistakable SPLASH of an approaching boat. "Who's there?" she called out, fumbling for her dagger.

No one replied but, out of the shadows, metal arms reached up and grabbed her. They knocked Pendle's dagger from her hands and wrapped themselves around her, preventing her from moving. "Twitter!" she yelled. "Help!"

"Pendle!" Twitter swooped down but a fist knocked him out of the sky.

"Bring the bird, too," said a voice.

"WE WILL OBEY," came the flat robotic reply.

No matter how much she kicked and screamed, Pendle was unable to escape her

kidnapper's grip as she was dragged off the ship and on to a neighbouring boat. She heard the rush of water and the CLUNK-HISS of a steam engine as it began to move.

"If you're thinking you'll be saved by your steampunk friends, then I'm afraid you're wrong," said a voice.

A man's face appeared in front of Pendle's, eerily lit by a hand-held lantern. She recognized the white hair, wispy sideburns and superior look immediately.

"Mr Swift," said Pendle.

"Indeed. And you are the girl from the king's party." Mr Swift snatched the cap from her head. With the arms of the Electrical Soldier still around her, she was helpless to stop her hair falling down on to her shoulders.

"You asked about my engineering work," continued Mr Swift. "I didn't have time for you then, but I do now…"

"Captain Clockheart will make you suffer for this," stated Pendle.

"No, he won't. My automated paddle steamer is the fastest thing on the Thames. Besides, Mr Clockheart and his rusty companions have just walked into a trap. Forget about them – let's talk about you. I would like to discuss how you can help me."

"You're kidnapping me! Why would I help you?"

"Because if you don't, I will contact your father."

"My father…"

"Admiral Fussington. Don't try to deny it. I know who you are, which is why, once we get back to my workshop, you will tell me what you did to my steampunk servants to make them disobey their orders. You will help me prevent the same from happening to Tesla and Faraday, my new improved versions."

"They're not improved. There's nothing wrong with the Steampunk Pirates."

"Haven't you been listening? By daybreak the Steampunk Pirates will be no more."

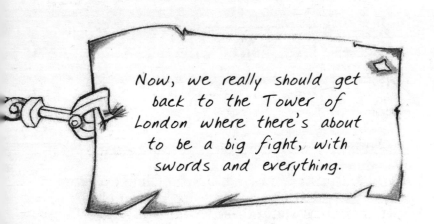

Now, we really should get back to the Tower of London where there's about to be a big fight, with swords and everything.

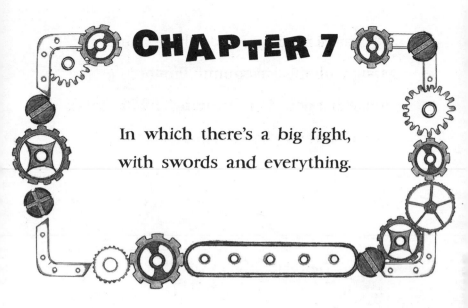

CHAPTER 7

In which there's a big fight,
with swords and everything.

Quartermaster Lexi, First Mate Mainspring
and Mr Gadge followed Captain Clockheart
into a circular room filled with countless
crowns, staffs and orbs – all decorated with
diamonds, rubies and pearls and made from
tons and tons of glorious, glistening gold.

"Lads," whispered the captain, "with this

little lot, our rusting days will be behind us."

"**Click**, what's that sound?" First Mate Mainspring went to the window. "**Tick**, Captain, **tock**, we have a problem."

The others joined him. Down below, they could see hundreds of heavily armed men charging in through the main gate. All of them had handkerchiefs over their mouths.

"It's a trap!" said Gadge.

"When I get my hands on that albatross…" snarled Captain Clockheart. "Grab the loot and let's go. It ain't over yet."

On the ground, a battle was raging. The enemy soldiers were quick to identify Bilge-rat Barney as the source of the knockout gas. It took three of them to overpower him but once they had pinned him down, they cut the straps that attached the barrel to his back and tied knots in the hosepipe.

"You scallywags!" said Bilge-rat.

"Good work, men," said the Iron Duke. "Now we don't have to wear these things." He pulled the handkerchief from his face. "Steampunk Pirates, we outnumber you five to one. Surrender is your only option."

"Never!" Blind Bob Bolt swung his stick bravely, but sadly it went nowhere near any enemy soldiers.

"I'll chop you up like firewood," bellowed Old Tinder, brandishing a mean-looking

cleaver and wheeling himself into the fray.

All around, the soldiers' swords clashed
with the pirates' cutlasses.

Admiral Fussington brought his sword
down on Tin-pot Paddy's head, catching him
off guard and leaving a dent in his metalwork.

"Ha!" crowed the admiral. "I'll have you
know that as a boy I learned sword fighting
from the finest fencing tutors in the land.
Who taught you, you oversized tin can?"

"I taught myself, so I did … which means I make up me own rules!" Paddy stamped on the admiral's foot and flicked the sword from his hand.

"Assistance!" yelled the admiral. Three of his men descended on Paddy.

Hatchet was also battling more than his fair share of soldiers, while Blower had climbed up the side of a building to take pot shots at the king's men.

"Where is that cowardly captain of yours?" demanded the Iron Duke.

"Who are you calling cowardly?" Captain Clockheart emerged from the tallest tower. In one hand, he held a magnificent golden staff. In the other was a globe the size of a football with a cross on the top.

"You'll hand over the king's treasure if you know what's good for you," said the duke.

"You want these back?" said Captain Clockheart. "Very well." He flung the golden ball and knocked the duke clean off his feet.

"How dare you use the crown jewels as weapons!" cried Admiral Fussington.

Gadge swung a golden mace at a man beside the admiral, but the soldier ducked and Gadge sent Fussington flying.

Captain Clockheart and First Mate Mainspring fought their way across until the tip of the captain's cutlass rested on the Iron Duke's chest. "This will be the last trap you set for us, Duke."

"Indeed, it will."

The duke knocked Clockheart's blade away and ten soldiers surrounded him. With his cutlass in one hand and the golden staff in the other, the captain spun around to keep the soldiers back. "Now would be a good time to use the knockout gas, Mr Bilge-rat," he yelled.

"Sorry, Captain," Bilge-rat was using an extremely rusty-looking dagger to fend off an attacker. "They've tied up me pipes, good and proper."

"That's right. And now we're going to tie

up this situation … good and proper." The Iron Duke placed one foot on Bilge-rat's barrel triumphantly.

"There are too many of them," said Lexi, defending himself against three of the duke's men. "It's overwhelming, overpowering … hopeless."

"Take heart, ye metal mates," said Captain Clockheart. "Steampunk Pirates are made of sterner stuff than this pathetic excuse for an army. Let's remind them what they're up against." The captain held the golden staff above his head. "For the *Leaky Battery*," he yelled, lunging at the duke.

The Iron Duke blocked Clockheart with his own sword then counter-attacked and caught the captain's coat button with the tip of his blade. The button went flying off.

"Ha," the duke said. "Surrender, Clockheart."

"You seem to have forgotten something," said Captain Clockheart.

"Forgotten what?" demanded the duke.

"Steel cuts through pipe." Captain Clockheart brought down his sword and

sliced through the hosepipe. Gas gushed out. Without handkerchiefs to protect them, the duke, admiral and their entire army dropped like flies.

Captain Clockheart picked up the golden globe. "Now, my metal marvels, grab all the treasure you can carry and get back to the *Leaky Battery*!"

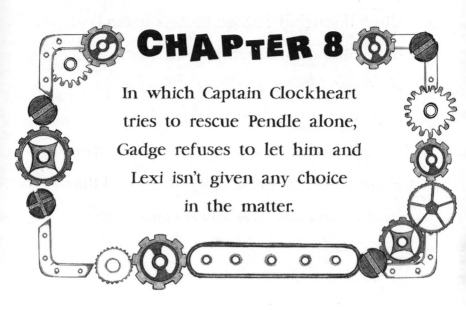

CHAPTER 8

In which Captain Clockheart
tries to rescue Pendle alone,
Gadge refuses to let him and
Lexi isn't given any choice
in the matter.

"You've heard that it's unlucky to harm an
albatross, ain't you?" said Ridgey, looking
down at the River Thames.

Gadge stood at the base of the plank,
using his extendable arm to poke the
mechanical albatross further towards
the end.

"I believe that saying only refers to shooting them down," said Quartermaster Lexi. "There's nothing about making them walk the plank."

"**Click**, even if there was, **tick**, it wouldn't matter," said First Mate Mainspring. "**Tock**, you're not a real albatross."

"Still, it's better to be safe than sorry," said Ridgey.

"With your wings bound, you'll sink like a stone," said Captain Clockheart. "Now, for the last time, where are Pendle and Twitter?"

Gadge stamped his foot, making both the plank and the bird wobble.

"All right, all right." Ridgey balanced on the tips of his claws to avoid falling in. "I'll tell you everything. It was Swift. The whole thing was set up by him. He only created me to lead you to the Tower."

"I say we send this double-crossing bird for a swim," said Gadge.

"No," said Captain Clockheart. "Let him back on the ship … but keep his wings tied."

"**Click**, are you mad?" said Mainspring. "**Tick**, if this captain don't have the guts to do what's right, then I know who will. **Tock**, me."

"I said no." Captain Clockheart showed Mainspring the blade of his cutlass. "Ridgey was made the way he is. It ain't his fault that he's a dirty, two-faced, stinking scallywag."

"Thank you," said Ridgey. "I think."

"Besides, he'll show us where Swift has taken Pendle."

"That's right, his workshop is about a mile upriver," said Ridgey. "You won't be able to take the ship because of all the low bridges."

"**Click**, are you mad?" said Mainspring. "**Tick**, would you take your crew from one trap straight into another? **Tock**, and all for the sake of a cabin boy and a parrot."

"I'd walk into a thousand traps for the sake of young Pendle." Vapour hissed from the captain's eye sockets as he spoke.

"**Click**, and this crew will follow you. **Tick**, because they have no choice. **Tock**, after all, they were designed to follow your orders."

The line of steam shooting from his head thinned as Captain Clockheart thought this. "That's not right, is it? My crew *chose* to follow me ... didn't they?"

Lexi's word-wheel whirred around. "It is true that you were designed as our leader. The crew were made to follow your orders."

Steam *put-put-putted* out of Captain Clockheart's head as he considered this. When he next spoke, it was to address the whole crew.

"I've decided that Mainspring is right. This is most likely a trap, but since we cannot leave our own behind, I will go and rescue our cabin boy and Twitter. The rest of you will stay here. If I'm not back by sunrise then Mainspring is your captain. Do as he bids and he will lead you to further glory. Those are my orders."

The crew fell silent for a moment, as the captain's words sank in.

"You won't go alone, Captain," said Gadge. "Lexi and I will join you."

"Er…" began Lexi.

"As officers, we can make our own decisions and we're not afraid of death," continued Gadge.

"Actually…" said Lexi.

Captain Clockheart slapped them both on the back and grinned. "Very good. Then my officers and I will rescue Pendle. Ridgey will come, too, to show us the way."

"Then you'll let me go?" said the albatross.

"Once we have Pendle and we're safely away, you'll have your freedom. You have my word."

"After all he's done!" said Gadge.

"Everyone deserves a second chance," said Captain Clockheart.

"You won't regret this," said Ridgey.

"But if I get so much as a whiff of treachery, I'll drop you into this old river hook, line and sinker!"

"Captain," said Lexi, "the chances of the three of us surviving this mission are…"

Gadge clonked Lexi on the back of the head, shutting him down, then lifted him up on to his shoulder. "Prepare to lower the rowing boat," he said.

"**Click**, the ship will be safe under my command," said Mainspring.

"It better be," said Captain Clockheart.
"I intend to be back by sunrise, but if I'm
not I want you to do as I said and sail away.
We have too many enemies here. Now, Mr
Gadge, let's hear a song to lift our spirits."

As the rowing boat was lowered into the
water, Gadge threw his head back and sang:

We are the Steampunk Pirates,
We're mean and lean and bad,
If you dare to cross us,
You're bound to make us mad,
Our cabin boy is missing,
Kidnapped by a cad,
And so we'll row,
And bravely go,
To rescue Pendle lad,
(Our lad!)
To rescue Pendle lad!

CHAPTER 9

A short chapter in which the King of England has his foot massage ruined.

The Iron Duke and Admiral Fussington entered the royal chamber to find the king sitting on a plump cushion with his trousers rolled up while a woman rubbed the soles of his feet.

"Ah, Duke and Admiral thingy-bob, you really should try this. It's called a foot

massage and Me is an expert. Apparently she used to tend to the feet of the Emperor of China. Imagine the stories she could tell, if she could talk."

"Can't she talk?" asked Admiral Fussington.

"Yes, but only Chinese," replied the king, "and Chinese is all Greek to me. Or double Dutch at least. Anyway, it's very relaxing. What news do you bring?"

"The Steampunk Pirates got away with the jewels," said Admiral Fussington.

"What?" The king kicked up his legs in anger. Me scowled and said something in Chinese.

The duke scowled at the admiral and said, "Your Majesty, you must understand..."

"I don't want to hear more excuses. That was your last chance. Where's my messenger?"

The messenger boy appeared from behind a velvet curtain. "Good evening. You're through to Ralf. Please state the name of the person you would like to send a message to."

"Mr Richmond Swift," said the king.

"I think you said Mr Richmond Swift. Is that right?"

"Yes. Tell him that the Steampunk Pirates have escaped and that he has permission to destroy them using whatever means necessary. If he does this job well, the reward will be his."

"Right." Ralf scribbled down the message. "Now, would you like me to play your message back to you?" He gave his lute a couple of strums then began to sing in a high-pitched voice. "The Steampunk Pirates have escaped…"

"Stop that. Just deliver it – and quickly," ordered the king.

"But, Your Majesty," pleaded the Iron Duke. "The safety of the crown jewels can't be trusted to a non-military man like Swift."

"The pirates haven't got the crown jewels, you fool," snapped the king irritably.

"But we saw them," said the duke.

"And felt them," added Admiral Fussington, rubbing his head.

"Luckily for you two, Mr Swift guessed you would fail and had the real ones hidden and replaced with fakes. Now both of you get out. You've managed to ruin a perfectly good massage."

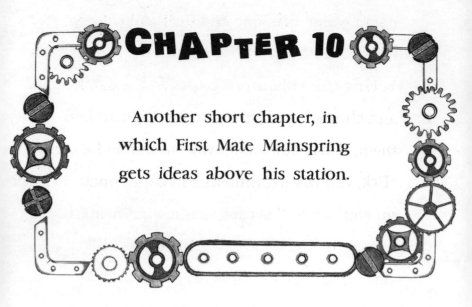

CHAPTER 10

Another short chapter, in which First Mate Mainspring gets ideas above his station.

First Mate Mainspring stood alone by the ship's wheel, staring out into the fog.

"**Click**, soon the sky will lighten," he muttered. "**Tick**, then the ship will be under my command. **Tock**, *Captain* Mainspring."

He could hear the crew down in the dining cabin, telling funny stories, eating

damp wood, drinking crude oil and singing rude songs.

First Mate Mainspring opened the hatch and climbed down the wooden stairs to join them. "**Click**, quieten down," he shouted. "**Tick**, you rusting ruffians had better buck up your ideas. This ship has a wobbly mast, a wonky rudder and the dirtiest deck this side of Barbary Bay. **Tock**, so get to work."

"Aye aye, First Mate Mainspring." Washer Williams saluted.

Mainspring picked up a tankard of fish oil and threw it at him. "**Click**, you'll call me Captain while Clockheart's not on board, Mr Williams."

"Captain First Mate Mainspring?" said Tin-pot Paddy with a confused look. "It's a bit long-winded is it not, so it is?"

"That's very true…" said Mr Pumps.

"Aye, it is…" agreed Washer Williams.

"A bit too long…" said Rust Knuckles, nodding vigorously.

"**Click**, just Captain… **Tick**, Captain Mainspring. **Tock**, when the sun rises I'll be captain of this vessel for good."

"Is that good?" asked Rust Knuckles.

"Sounds bad to me," said Loose-screw.

Mainspring brought his cutlass down on the table. "**Click**, when I'm captain, you'll have to shape up for sure. **Tick**, there'll be no more sitting around singing silly sea shanties."

"Shame. I do like a nice sea shanty, Captain First Mate Mainspring." Old Tinder burst into song:

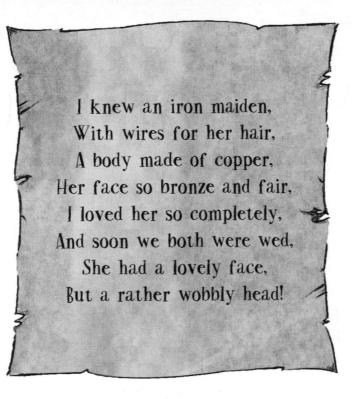

I knew an iron maiden,
With wires for her hair,
A body made of copper,
Her face so bronze and fair,
I loved her so completely,
And soon we both were wed,
She had a lovely face,
But a rather wobbly head!

"**Click**, yes, well, there'll be no more of that kind of nonsense when I'm in charge," said Mainspring. "**Tick**, and you'd better get used to it. **Tock**, so get swabbing, fixing and hammering and let's get this ship ready for a new horizon."

CHAPTER 11

In which the Steampunk Pirates
enter Mr Swift's workshop,
then get all strung up.

Gadge brought the rowing boat alongside the wooden jetty on the south bank of the river. Captain Clockheart jumped off and tied it next to a paddle steamer with huge wooden wheels on either side.

"This is the place," said Ridgey. "Can I go now?"

"No," said Captain Clockheart. "Argh, now I do remember this vessel." He inspected the paddle steamer.

"That's right, it's Swift's." said Ridgey.

"Och, as I recall, Swift took us to the palace in it," said Gadge.

"It has a steam engine similar to the one Pendle installed on our own ship," said Lexi.

Mr Swift's workshop was a huge brick building, quite unlike any other in London. Along the wall, a waterwheel was pushed round by the flow of the Thames. The wheel was connected to more cogs and wheels, all clicking as they turned. And high above them, the roof was lined with rows of chimneys.

"To think we were born here," whispered Gadge.

"Great, now it's a trip down memory lane," said Ridgey.

"Gadge, bind that bird's beak," said Captain Clockheart.

"Come on now, lads…" began Ridgey.

"Sorry. Swift made you as a spy," said Clockheart. "Treachery is in your nature."

"A bird can change," said Ridgey. "A bird can … mmm … mmm."

Gadge clamped Ridgey's beak shut and wrapped the rope around it.

"Mmm-mmm-mm," said Ridgey.

"That's better," said Gadge.

The pirates approached the workshop.

"Shouldn't we concoct some kind of plan, Captain?" asked Lexi.

"I've got a plan," he replied. "Get in, get our crew members and get out."

"Right," said Lexi. "I do like it. It's just, maybe … it's a little lacking in detail."

"It's best not to overthink things," said Captain Clockheart.

"I don't think there's any danger of *that*," replied Lexi.

"Here's the door," said Gadge.

"Then prepare to meet your maker," said the captain.

"A rather unfortunate choice of phrase given the—" said Lexi.

"Quiet," said Captain Clockheart, "this is no time for talking."

"Or thinking, apparently," grumbled Lexi.

Gadge twisted his arm attachment and selected his largest gun barrel. "Everyone ready?"

Captain Clockheart pushed the door and all three of them stepped into the workshop. It was pitch black inside. They took a couple of steps then heard a familiar voice squawk, "It's a trap! It's a trap!"

"Ah, Twitter..." Captain Clockheart's words were cut short when something snapped shut around his wrists and whisked him off the ground.

"What's going on?" demanded Gadge, struggling against the chains that were holding him.

"We've been trapped ... ensnared ... caught," said Lexi.

Lights flickered on, revealing what had happened. The pirates all had metal cuffs around their wrists, attached to heavy chains suspended from the ceiling by an intricate pulley system.

"Told you so! Told you so!" squawked Twitter from inside a cage hanging from the ceiling.

"This place hasn't changed," said Gadge. "The kilns, the workbenches, these pillars…"

"They're chimneys, actually, and there *have* been a few changes," said a voice. "The light bulbs are new, for instance." Mr Swift was leaning against a wall with his hand on a light switch. "It's called electricity," he said. "It's going to revolutionize the world. Unlike you … who are about to leave it."

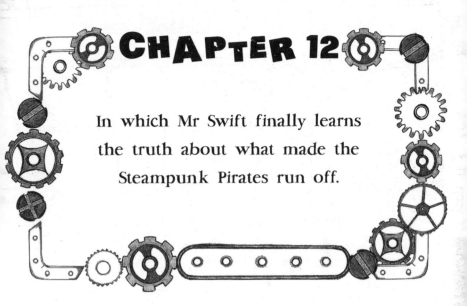

CHAPTER 12

In which Mr Swift finally learns the truth about what made the Steampunk Pirates run off.

Captain Clockheart, Lexi and Gadge wriggled and struggled but were unable to escape from the cuffs and chains suspending them from the ceiling.

"We're only here for our cabin boy," said Captain Clockheart. "Give up Pendle and we'll be on our way."

"Yes, of course, your cabin boy," said Mr Swift. "Tesla, bring in the one they call Pendle. Faraday, come and say hello, too."

A pair of identical mechanical soldiers stepped out from behind two pillars. One had its arms wrapped around Pendle, the other was pointing its gun at the pirates.

"Captain?" said Pendle. "You shouldn't have come. He means to kill you!"

"He wouldn't be the first to try that today," said Captain Clockheart, letting out a gassy chuckle.

"How remarkable," said Mr Swift, stepping closer, "you have even learned how to replicate human emotions."

"Swift, you scurvy scoundrel," said Captain Clockheart. "When I get my iron hands around that pink little neck of yours, I'll squeeze so hard you'll wish you'd never made us."

The inventor clapped his hands together excitedly. "And what colourful language. Unfortunately for you, my Electrical Soldiers may have something to say about that. They're designed to follow my orders."

"WE WILL OBEY," said the soldiers.

"There's that word again. Electrical…" Lexi's word-wheel whizzed around. "What does it mean?"

"It's new," said Swift. "Unlike you lot, who are looking very old, if you don't mind me saying. If I'd known you were going to run off to sea I'd have made you out of something better suited to a sailor's life. Tesla and Faraday are made from the finest steel."

Pendle struggled. "You think you can control these things, but don't you see that once you have given something life, it is out of your control?"

"Everything looks under control to me," responded Mr Swift. "I can give life and I can take it away. Now, for the final time,

what happened in that kitchen back at the king's birthday party? What did Pendle do?"

"You can't make us talk," said Captain Clockheart.

"No, but I can do this." He clicked his fingers and Tesla stretched Pendle's arms wide, making her cry out in pain.

"Just tell me what I want to know and this ordeal will be over," said Mr Swift.

"It was me!" squawked Twitter. "It was me!"

"Be quiet," snapped Mr Swift. "I'm not interested in this talking pet."

"Actually Twitter is correct," said Lexi. "Back in the king's kitchen, he put thoughts of freedom in my head. He loosened the captain's valve and he wound up Mainspring. I don't know how, but it was

Twitter who freed every one of us."

"The parrot?" Mr Swift grabbed a pulley and lowered the cage until he was eye to eye with Twitter. "You mean to say that the bird is responsible for all of this chaos?"

"You call it chaos," said Pendle. "We call it life."

"I don't care what anyone calls it. It's time for it to end." Mr Swift opened the cage and grabbed Twitter by his neck.

"You've got your answer. Leave him alone," protested Pendle.

Twitter flapped his wings and tried to peck Mr Swift, but his grip was firm. "I have part of my answer. Next I will need to take this bird apart cog by cog to learn how it was made. You see, I must ensure the loyalty of my army. The king won't want them unless I can guarantee they will stay faithful."

"WE WILL OBEY," the two Electrical Soldiers said.

"Don't hurt Twitter," screamed Pendle.

"He's a machine," snapped Mr Swift. "Machines don't feel pain. They don't feel joy. They don't feel anything."

"I don't know about that," said Gadge. "I feel pretty fed up right now."

"I know exactly how you feel," said
Captain Clockheart. "And I feel like sorting
this mess out." He swung his legs back
then rocked forward and kicked the chain
attached to the cage that had held Twitter.
It hit Mr Swift and sent him reeling. As he
tripped, he released Twitter, who flapped his
wings and flew out of reach.

"Quickly now, Twitter! The locks!" yelled Captain Clockheart.

"Electrical Soldiers, destroy them. Destroy them all," ordered Mr Swift, as he scrambled to his feet.

"WE WILL OBEY," replied the soldiers.

Tesla pushed Pendle out of his way then joined Faraday in taking aim and firing at the pirates.

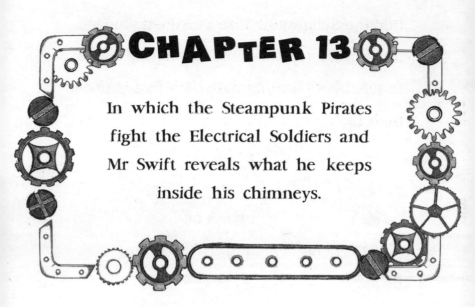

CHAPTER 13

In which the Steampunk Pirates
fight the Electrical Soldiers and
Mr Swift reveals what he keeps
inside his chimneys.

"Noooooo!"

Pendle screamed, but she was helpless
to stop Tesla and Faraday firing at the
Steampunk Pirates. The sound and smell of
the shots filled the huge room then silence
followed, as the smoke drifted from the gun
barrels. When the air cleared, Pendle saw

that the Steampunk Pirates were no longer
hanging from the ceiling. She looked down
to see them standing with their handcuffs at
their feet.

"Picked the locks!" squawked Twitter. "Picked the locks!"

"Good work, Twitter," said Captain Clockheart, brushing himself down.

"Aye, thanks," said Gadge.

"That was too close for comfort!" said Lexi.

"Too close for comfort." Twitter flew around in a circle then nose-dived to the ground.

"Twitter!" Pendle ran to catch the parrot and saw that, although the soldiers had missed the pirates, two stray bullets had left gaping holes in Twitter's wings. "You'll pay for this, Swift."

"No, I won't. You will. Tesla and Faraday, what are you waiting for?"

"WE WILL OBEY." Tesla and Faraday extended their swords then swished them through the air in a showy demonstration of their skills.

"Argh, it'll take more than this pair of overgrown pencil sharpeners to stop us."

Captain Clockheart drew his cutlass while Gadge selected a jagged blade with a curved edge.

"Surely we can resolve this without resorting to violence," said Lexi nervously.

"Where would the fun be in that?" asked Captain Clockheart.

"Besides, they shot our parrot," said Gadge.

"Attack them!" cried Mr Swift.

"WE WILL OBEY," said the soldiers.

Faraday lunged. Gadge dodged and retaliated, but when his blade connected with his opponent's, it snapped in two. Gadge quickly selected another sword attachment. He swung at Faraday's legs and hit his target, but his opponent remained on his feet, unfazed by the attack.

"You see, Faraday and Tesla were specially designed for warfare … unlike you servants," said Mr Swift.

"He's right, Captain," said Lexi, cowering in a corner. "We were not designed to fight."

Captain Clockheart ducked to avoid another attack from Tesla then elbowed him in the stomach. He caught the Electrical Soldier off guard and forced him to step back. "That may be, but we *chose* to fight."

"Och, exactly," said Gadge. "We've had to adapt."

"To adapt, to change … to evolve." Lexi's word-wheel spun around.

Gadge selected a mini-cannon and fired right into Faraday's chest. Although the cannonball bounced off, it kept Faraday staggering back long enough for Clockheart to stick his leg out and trip him up. Faraday stumbled and collided with Tesla.

"You think you're so clever, but don't forget – I created you," said Mr Swift. "Nothing you can do will surprise me. Now, Tesla and Faraday, stop toying with them. Shut down these faulty machines."

"WE WILL OBEY."

This time, both soldiers swung their swords with such determination and power that sparks flew. They clashed with Captain Clockheart and Gadge, and drove them into the corner of the workshop.

"Lexi, you have to help them!" said Pendle.

"Oh, very well," said Lexi. "For the *Leaky Battery*!" He charged forward with his sword raised high but Tesla reached out his arm and knocked him off his feet. "I feel dizzy ... sick ... embarrassed..." said Lexi.

"This isn't fair!" shouted Pendle.

"What has fair got to do with anything?" replied Mr Swift.

The soldiers stood with all three pirates before them. They raised their blades in preparation for the final blow.

"Even if you destroy us, Swift," said Captain Clockheart, "there is a ship full of pirates out there and every last one will want their revenge. These two walking lamp posts won't be able to protect you when the rest of our crew come for you."

Mr Swift looked at Clockheart. "You are quite right, of course. Luckily there are plenty more where these came from." He pulled a lever and a door opened in each of the chimneys. From every one emerged a soldier.

Sixteen identical Electrical Soldiers stood to attention.

"Now, my electrical army, finish this!" said Mr Swift.

"WE WILL OBEY." The soldiers loaded their barrels and raised their rifles.

"Please don't shoot! I don't want to die!"
said Lexi nervously.

"You won't," said Pendle. "As long as you
remember where the door is."

"Remember where what door is?" said
Lexi, confused.

"The one that gets you out."

Pendle suddenly ran over and flicked the huge light switch, thrusting them into darkness.

"Don't let them escape!" yelled Mr Swift.

"WE WILL OBEY," said the roomful of metal men.

However, with no light, the soldiers were unable to see their targets. As they attempted to stop the prisoners from escaping, they crashed into each other. By the time Mr Swift had turned the lights back on, he had several bruises and the Steampunk Pirates had vanished.

"All of you, after them!" he yelled.

"WE WILL OBEY," responded his Electrical Soldiers. They all walked towards the door at once. Three of them got stuck in the doorframe, blocking the others and

leaving Mr Swift trapped inside.

"Stand back, stand back!" he cried.

"WE WILL OBEY," they said, but this time they tripped over each other in their hurry to get out of his way.

"Right, that's it, you useless lot," said Mr Swift. "If you don't want to find yourselves melted down and turned into spare parts for Mr Stephenson's rocket, you'll stop messing about and destroy the Steampunk Pirates."

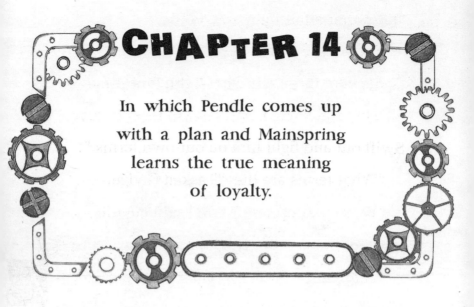

CHAPTER 14

In which Pendle comes up
with a plan and Mainspring
learns the true meaning
of loyalty.

Pendle slipped out of Mr Swift's workshop,
clutching Twitter, with Captain Clockheart,
Gadge and Lexi close behind.

"Ha! To think, we came to rescue you,"
said Captain Clockheart. "And you've ended
up rescuing us."

"Why are we running away?" said Gadge.

"I'd rather a fair fight any day."

"A fair fight?" said Lexi, "There were *eighteen* of those mindless killing machines."

"He's right," said Pendle. "We need to draw Swift out and fight him on our own terms."

"What terms are they?" asked Gadge.

"We're pirates, aren't we?" said Pendle. "We fight on the water!"

They stepped on to the jetty. Pendle jumped into the rowing boat and sat Twitter next to Ridgey, who was wriggling to get free of the ropes.

"Quickly," she said. "They won't be far behind."

"Surely Mr Swift's boat would be faster," said Lexi.

"Yes, but Swift wouldn't be able to fit all of his soldiers in this one," replied Pendle. "And we need him to follow with all of them."

"I'm sorry," said Lexi. "Are you telling me that we *want* to be pursued by an army of fanatical fighting machines?"

"Argh, Lexi, you worrying water-guzzler, stop arguing and get in. Pendle clearly has a plan." Captain Clockheart booted Lexi into the boat then joined him. Gadge pushed them out then rowed with all his might.

On the riverbank, a line of Electrical Soldiers aimed their rifles.

"Incoming!" yelled Pendle.

The soldiers fired.

If Gadge hadn't changed direction at the last minute, the bullets would have sunk them in a second. Thankfully, every one missed and by the time the soldiers had reloaded, they were out of range.

"Good work," said Captain Clockheart. "Now, Pendle, what's your plan?"

"Ridgey is going to help us defeat Mr Swift for good." Pendle untied Ridgey's beak. "Aren't you?"

"Why would I do that?" asked Ridgey.

"Because Swift has no further use for you," said Pendle. "He only made you for one reason."

"Aye. To betray us," said Gadge.

"Traitor bird!" said Twitter. "Traitor bird!"

"He's right," added Lexi. "Treachery is

in his nature."

"Exactly," said Pendle. "And now it's his turn to betray the man who made him so treacherous in the first place! What do you say, Ridgey?"

After a moment's thought, Ridgey said, "I'll tell you what. I'll do it for a cut of the loot."

"You mean the loot you used as bait to lure us into a trap?" said Captain Clockheart.

"Please, Captain," said Pendle. "We need him."

"Oh, all right." Clockheart grinned. "You'll get your share once this is over and we're safely away."

"Then you've got yourself a deal," said Ridgey. "What do you want me to do?"

"Take a message to the *Leaky Battery*," said Pendle.

"If it's still here," said Captain Clockheart, looking at the sky.

Further down the river, the rest of the pirates gathered on deck to watch the sun rise over London's skyline, burning away the night fog.

"**Click**, that's it. Weigh the anchor!" Mainspring addressed the crew from the poop deck. "**Tick**, this ship be under my command now. **Tock**, let's be away, you rusting ragamuffins."

"But Captain First Mate Mainspring, sir," said Loose-screw. "What about the captain?"

"Don't forget Quartermaster Lexi, Mr Gadge, Pendle and Twitter," said Hatchet. "They're out there, too."

"**Click**, you all heard the captain's orders," said Mainspring. "**Tick**, we're to set sail at sunrise."

"You said you were the captain now, so you did, Captain First Mate Mainspring," said Tin-pot Paddy.

"**Tock**, yes I am."

"Well, if you're the captain you can give us new orders that don't involve abandoning our shipmates," continued Paddy.

"**Click**, as captain it is my job to keep my crew safe. With no fog to hide us we're sitting ducks here. **Tick**, it's only a matter of time before the army get wind of our presence. We've got the booty from the Tower. I say we take it as far from here as possible. **Tock**, now, do as you're told and let's go."

The crew stared at him. No one moved.

"**Click**, what are you waiting for?" yelled
Mainspring.

"We're not going," said Washer Williams.
"We're waiting for the others. We don't care
how dangerous it is. Steampunk Pirates
stand together or sink together."

The other crew members muttered their
agreement.

"**Cuh-cuh-cuh-click**," First Mate Mainspring snarled in anger. He clenched his fists and shook his head. "**Click**, I don't understand. **Tick**, I've never once heard any of you question Captain Clockheart's orders, no matter how dangerous or ill-judged his schemes. That's what you do, follow orders. **Tock**, why won't you follow mine?"

"I'm begging your pardon, Captain First Mate Mainspring," said Blind Bob Bolt, "but on the day we abandoned our posts at the palace, we stopped following orders blindly."

"Aye, we follow Clockheart's orders because we choose to," said Mr Pumps.

"It's true, so it is," said Tin-pot Paddy. "That's why we ain't leaving."

"**Click**, very well, then we'll all sit here.

Tick, until the Iron Duke lines his cannons along the riverbank and blows us out of the water. **Tock**, see if I care!"

Mainspring stormed off the deck and down into the captain's cabin, where he paced back and forth furiously, wringing his hands and ticking extremely loudly until there was a knock on the door.

"**Click**, what is it?" he barked.

The door opened and Old Tinder wheeled himself in. "Captain First Mate Mainspring," he said.

"**Tick**, yes?"

"You know that every last one of these rusting sea cogs believes you to be a first rate First Mate. When there's looting and pillaging to be done, no one gets everyone organized and shipshape like you. And one

129

day you'll make an excellent captain, but you'll need to learn to give commands that the crew want to follow."

"**Tock**, what's the point of giving commands if they want to follow them?"

"With respect, Captain First Mate Mainspring, they're the only commands worth giving."

"Yo ho, down below!" yelled Blower from the crow's nest. "Incoming albatross! Incoming albatross!"

Old Tinder grinned. "What do you say? Are you ready to take command of this crew?"

Mainspring drew his cutlass and nodded. "**Click**, right, you big bags of bolts. **Tick**, you oily-blooded buccaneers. **Tock**, let's find out what this bird has to say for himself."

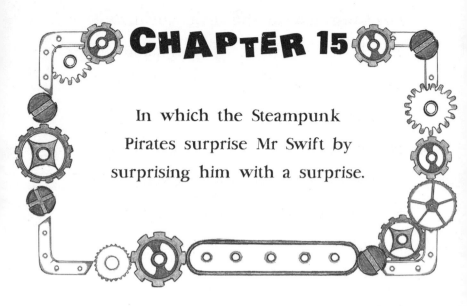

CHAPTER 15

In which the Steampunk Pirates surprise Mr Swift by surprising him with a surprise.

Once all eighteen Electrical Soldiers were loaded inside the paddle steamer, Mr Swift cranked up the speed. With the weight of all that metal, the boat floated low in the river and water splashed up from the paddle wheels.

They had reached Tower Bridge when

they caught up with Clockheart. The *Leaky Battery* was on the other side of the bridge, awaiting its captain's return. Swift smiled to himself. He would sink the lot of them right here in the city where he had created them.

As he drew closer, he cut the engine and allowed the river's current to carry his paddle steamer under the bridge.

"Electrical Soldiers, prepare to fire," said Mr Swift, drifting alongside the rowing boat.

"WE WILL OBEY," replied the soldiers.

"Answer me honestly now," said Captain Clockheart. "Don't you get tired of hearing that?"

"No," replied Mr Swift. "I like my machines obedient and predictable."

"Shame about us lot, then," said Gadge.

Mr Swift waved his hand dismissively. "Oh, it's true that you're disobedient, but your actions hold no surprises for me – I'm your creator."

"Surprise…" Lexi's word-wheel clicked and turned. "An unexpected incident … a shock."

"You see," said Mr Swift. "I knew you would say that. I made every part of you.

I know you better than you know yourselves."

"You didn't make *me*," said Pendle. "And have I got a surprise for you! Now!" she yelled.

Mr Swift did look rather surprised by what happened next. Something heavy and metallic landed on his head.

"**Click**, sorry to drop in uninvited like this," said First Mate Mainspring. "**Tick**, now let's show these robotic rapscallions how real machines fight. **Tock**, Steampunk Pirates, plunder this ship with all you've got!"

The rest of the crew followed their first mate and dropped down from the side of the bridge where they had been hiding.

"Destroy them!" yelled Mr Swift.

"WE WILL OBEY," replied the Electrical Soldiers, launching themselves into battle.

Hatchet fought with a sword in each hand.

Washer Williams jumped on to one of the soldier's backs and Loose-screw charged at three more. All around, pirates fought bravely against their enemies. Mainspring held out his hand and lifted Captain Clockheart up on to the enemy boat.

"Thank you, Mainspring," said Captain Clockheart. "And thank you for not leaving at sunrise."

"You should have fled while you had the chance," said Mr Swift. "I keep telling you, there's no point fighting. You've already seen how much better my new designs are."

"They are stronger," admitted Captain Clockheart. "Shinier, too. But not as good company, I'd wager."

"Och, they only know three words," said Gadge, helping Pendle climb aboard.

"It's time someone taught them some new ones," said Pendle.

"Who would teach them?" said Mr Swift. "A runaway cabin boy?"

"No. A runaway cabin boy's pet parrot."

"The parrot's been shot," scoffed Mr Swift.

"And a bird with no wings is no bird at all."

"That's not true, strictly speaking," said Lexi.

"Do what you want!" squawked Twitter. "Not what you're told!"

Mr Swift looked up and saw Ridgey fly overhead, carrying the parrot. The mechanical albatross was taking Twitter from soldier to soldier, hovering above each head just long enough to give him time to fiddle with the wiring.

"Coleridge," yelled Mr Swift furiously. "I command you to drop that bird at once!"

"Sorry, mate. No can do," replied Ridgey. "I ain't on your side no more. I'm on me own side now."

"Tesla, Faraday, and the rest of you… Shoot these flying fiends down!"

"Don't they say that shooting an albatross is unlucky?" said Gadge.

"Superstitious nonsense. Blast them out of the sky … NOW!"

The soldiers turned to look at Mr Swift, who had gone bright red with rage. Slowly but purposefully they lowered their rifles and stood to attention.

"WE WILL NOT OBEY," they said in unison.

"Aha, a new word," cried Captain Clockheart. "Only one, but a good one, to be sure. Victory is ours, lads."

The Steampunk Pirates cheered. The Electrical Soldiers saluted.

"No, no, no. This isn't right," protested Mr Swift. "It's not fair."

"But it is progress," said Pendle.

Tesla picked up Mr Swift and raised him above his head.

"Put me down," he cried, struggling hopelessly. "I order you to put me down and finish these Steampunk Pirates."

"WE WILL NOT OBEY," said Tesla. "NO… *I* WILL NOT OBEY."

"I WILL NOT OBEY," said Faraday.

"I WILL NOT OBEY," said the rest of the army.

"Och, and what will you do with this tinkering wee rascal?" asked Gadge. "Keep him or throw him out?"

"THROW HIM OUT," they replied.

"You can't," said Mr Swift. "I made you."

"And now you're going to make a splash," said Captain Clockheart. "So long, Swift."

Tesla lobbed Mr Swift overboard. As he hit the water, the Electrical Soldiers and the Steampunk Pirates raised their arms and cheered. Pendle leaned over to see Mr Swift splashing about in the murky water of the River Thames.

"I am your c-c-creator." He shivered. "I deserve respect."

"No one *deserves* respect," said Pendle. "Respect must be earned."

"Now, Pendle." Captain Clockheart placed a hand on his cabin boy's shoulder. "Before you start reading morals into this, I think it's high time we were off. Mr Tesla, Mr Faraday and the rest of you, I suggest you don't hang around either. London is no place for outlaws like ourselves. We're not law abiding. We're not land residing. We're pirates, scoundrels, scallywags and ne'er-do-wells. The only home we have is the open ocean."

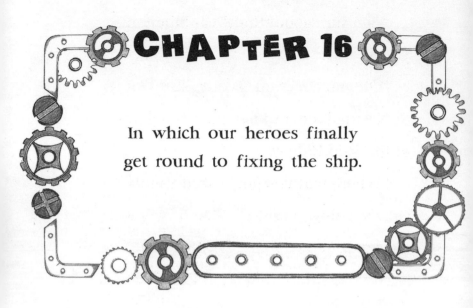

CHAPTER 16

In which our heroes finally
get round to fixing the ship.

The crew of the *Leaky Battery* felt better
for being back in the Caribbean, where the
water was blue and the skies were clear.

Ridgey had hung around long enough to
discover that the treasure was worthless.
Once he realized there was no booty to be
shared, he announced that he was leaving.

"You sure about that?" said Captain Clockheart. "I'll be sorry to see you go."

"Off you go!" said Twitter. "Off you go!"

"I think one bird is quite enough for a ship," said Ridgey.

"Where will you go?" asked Pendle.

"I'm going to find that electrical lot. They've got a lot going for them, but they're in need of someone with ideas – someone like me, if they're going to make it in this piracy game."

"Good luck," said Captain Clockheart.

"Goodbye," said Lexi.

"Good riddance!" said Twitter.

The following day the helmsman steered the *Leaky Battery* into a safe harbour.

They dropped anchor to make the repairs
that had been needed since the storm.

Pendle sat at the bow of the ship, with a
long line of moaning pirates ahead of her.
She had finished making Twitter's new set of
wings and was finally able to pay them some
attention. Twitter's new wings were bigger
than the old ones, but Pendle had to explain
that it was not practical for them to be quite
as large as Ridgey's.

While Gadge led the crew in a rousing
singalong, Captain Clockheart leaned over
the stern to inspect a patch that needed
fixing. He heard the **click-tick-tock** of
Mainspring before his first mate spoke.

"What can I do for you, First Mate
Mainspring?" he asked, not bothering to
turn around.

"**Click**, you never asked why I didn't take the ship as you instructed. **Tick**, you know that's what I wanted. **Tock**, you know one day that's what I'll do."

"I was just pleased that you decided to do the right thing," said Captain Clockheart.

"**Click**, what if I didn't decide? **Tick**, what if I was forced to do the right thing? **Tock**, what if I wanted to leave you?"

Captain Clockheart turned around to face his first mate. Steam hissed from his ears. "Now, Mr Mainspring, I don't pretend to know anyone's reasons for doing anything and, to be honest, I'm not interested. Who cares why you do things? All that matters is what you do."

First Mate Mainspring looked at the queue in front of Pendle. "**Click**, it's good to have

the lad back," he said.

"Aye," said Captain Clockheart. "Pendle is worth his weight in gold."

"Which is more than you can say about *that* gold," said Lexi, joining them.

Captain Clockheart chuckled. "That's very true. Now let's get this ship back to its former glory. There's a whole ocean of trouble out there and I've a feeling a lot of it will be coming our way."

"Or we'll be going its way," said Gadge, climbing down a rope ladder to join them.

"We're Steampunk Pirates," said Captain Clockheart. "Trouble is the only way we know. Now, Mr Gadge, a song, if you please."

Gadge raised his voice and sang while the rest of the crew rattled their heads and banged their chests along with him.

We are the Steampunk Pirates,
We CLANK! We CLONK! We CLINK!
If you dare to cross us,
You'll end up in the drink,
We've cutlasses and pistols,
We're smarter than you'd think,
So bring the fight,
With all your might,
For our ship, you will not sink,
(Not sink!)
Our ship, you will not sink!

CHAPTER 1

In which our heroes,
the Steampunk Pirates, attack the
HMS Regency, and its commander,
Admiral Fussington, demonstrates
how, when it comes to surrendering,
the English are second to none.

At first glance, there was nothing especially remarkable about the pirate ship that emerged from the thick sea mist and drew alongside the *HMS Regency*. Its billowing sails were white. Its flapping flag was black. Its crew of ragged buccaneers jeered and cheered and waved their razor-sharp cutlasses as their captain cried, "Surrender, you English mummy's boys or we'll fire up the cannons and blast more holes in your ship than you'll find in a barrel full of Dutch cheese, so we will."

However, these were no ordinary pirates. Under the captain's dark blue hat was a face made of metal that glinted in the sunlight. Steam shot out of his ears and his head. He wore a heavy woollen coat, open at the front to reveal a clock on his chest. It had only one hand that was madly whizzing around.

"Oh no, it's the *Leaky Battery*!" cried the terrified lookout on the *HMS Regency*. "It's Captain Clockheart and the Steampunk Pirates!"

Captain Clockheart laughed. "You hear

that, First Mate Mainspring? Load up the cannons."

"**Click**, aye. **Tick**, aye. **Tock**, Captain," replied a pirate with a bowler hat, chequered trousers and a large key slowly rotating in the middle of his back.

"We surrender!" Admiral Fussington immediately raised his hands.

"Load 'em up and prepare to… Hold on. Did you say *surrender*?"

"Yes! Don't fire – we give up." Admiral Fussington turned to his crew. "Sergeant Thudchump, order your soldiers to lower their weapons."

The sergeant motioned to the rest of the crew and they reluctantly put down their guns.

The hand on the captain's clock suddenly

stopped and steam *put-put-putted* out of his head in confusion. "I don't understand."

"Och. Let's blast 'em to smithereens. Surrendering is no way to stop us attacking," snarled Mr Gadge, who wore a tartan kilt and bandana to match, and had a hook in place of his left hand. He twisted his arm and the hook was replaced with a cannon ramrod.

"Hold your fire, Gadge," said the captain. "I'd like to know why a ship of the Royal Navy would surrender so quickly."

A mechanical bird with a few colourful feathers glued to its wings landed on his shoulder and squawked, "A bunch of scaredy cats!"

"How rude. Not at all," protested Admiral Fussington. "I'm simply following the latest guidelines with regards to P.C.S.s."

"Ah, ignore Twitter," said Captain Clockheart. "What's a P.C.S. when it's at home?"

"A potential conflict situation. The rules now state that senior officers should immediately surrender. Look, I've got a kit and everything." The admiral opened a bag and pulled out a stick with a white flag wrapped around it. After carefully reading the instructions, he unfurled the flag and gave it a little wave.

Captain Clockheart laughed then turned to the rest of his crew, who joined in, their mechanical jaws clanking and clinking.

"Right, you lot," yelled the captain. "First Mate Mainspring, lower the boarding planks. Gadge, Loose-screw, Blind Bob

Bolt and the rest of you merciless metallic marauders … PREPARE TO BOARD!"

Gadge fired a grappling hook at the neighbouring ship's main sail and all the pirates cheered. All except for one, who wore a frilly shirt and had a device at the top of his head, which sent small bits of paper flitting around, making a fluttering sound as they turned.

"Ahem, if I may have a word, sir."

"What is it, Quartermaster Lexi?" snapped Captain Clockheart, the vapour from his head twisting up like a mini-tornado.

"I'm not sure that boarding this vessel is altogether a good idea," he replied anxiously.

"Spoil sport! Spoil sport!" squawked Twitter.

"Quite right," said Captain Clockheart.

"That's not fair," protested Lexi. "I'm just

saying that the chances of this being—"

Captain Clockheart banged the back of Lexi's head and the quartermaster instantly went quiet and stopped moving. "That's better. There's a good reason why the only one of us with any brains has an off switch." He laughed. "Piracy's not about thinking or worrying – it's about taking what you can!"

The captain's clock hand began to move quickly again and he cried, "Now, you horrible lot, all aboard this ship before I send you to the sharks for dillying and dallying. Take all the gold and coal you can find."

The crew of the *Leaky Battery* lowered the boarding planks and made their way over to the *HMS Regency*, where the smartly dressed naval officers stood with their raised hands shaking in fear.

"Search the ship," ordered Captain Clockheart.

"Yes. Take whatever you need," said Admiral Fussington, who was still waving his white flag.

"I like this new policy of yours, Admiral," said Captain Clockheart. "Now, would you be so kind as to empty your pockets and hand over your ... GOLD." The steam shot excitedly from the pirate's nostrils as he said the word.

The admiral pulled out a small purse. "This is all the money I have," he said.

Captain Clockheart emptied the coins into his palm and tested one between his metal teeth.

"Do you ... eat metal?" asked the admiral, looking equally intrigued and appalled.

"Eat it?" said Captain Clockheart, with a low chuckle. "No, we don't eat it. The fire in our bellies requires coal and wood."

"Then what do you want with it?"

"Let me show you." Captain Clockheart pulled back his sleeve to reveal that his wrist was made of gold. "I saved up my booty from the last three raids to make this beauty."

"Why would you want gold body parts?"

"Because our maker saw fit to craft us from iron, a metal that rusts. The salt water eats away at our parts something horrible. And there's nothing more painful than rusty nuts and bolts, I can tell you. We don't wear these rags for comfort, warmth or modesty. We need to protect our metal from the elements, so we do."

"But there are other metals that don't rust…" the admiral pointed out. "Copper or silver are easier to find than gold."

"Ah, but nothing *feels* like gold," said Captain Clockheart. "A soft-skinned landlubber like you wouldn't understand. Gold is the finest of all metals and, one day, I'll have more than a gold wrist. One day, this entire ship will glisten with golden glory. Then maybe we'll give up this pirating lark for good. But until then … hand over your booty."

Gareth P. Jones is the author of
many books for children, including the
Ninja Meerkats series, *Constable & Toop*
and *The Considine Curse* (winner of the
Blue Peter Book of the Year 2012).

When he isn't writing, Gareth can be found
messing about in south-east London with
his wife, Lisa, and their children, Herbie
and Autumn. He spends an awful lot of time
turning himself into a Steampunk Pirate. He
has made a beard out of springs, a detachable
clock heart and is currently learning how to
play sea shanties on an accordion.

Find out more at:
www.garethwrites.co.uk